Biff's carpet was torn. It had a big hole in it.
Biff showed Dad but he said,
   "We can't afford a new one. Sorry, Biff."

Biff and Chip were shopping with Dad. Dad wanted to buy a bookcase for Kipper's room. They saw one outside the junk shop.

"I'll get this for Kipper," said Dad.

Biff found an old carpet in the back of the shop.
"This would do for my room," she said.
She asked Dad if she could have it.

Dad looked at the old carpet.

"You don't want that thing," he said. "It's old and dirty."

"But I like it," said Biff. "Please may I have it?" So Dad said, "Yes, as long as it doesn't cost too much."

Biff beat the carpet. It was full of dust and dirt.
"I didn't think a carpet could be so dusty,"
she said. "I wonder who had it last. Someone who
didn't wipe their feet!"

Biff and Mum gave the carpet a shampoo.
"I don't think it has ever had a shampoo
before," said Biff. "It looks better already."

The carpet looked beautiful.

"It is a nice carpet," said Biff, "I told you so!
It looks quite old, so maybe it's worth a lot of
money."

Biff was in her bedroom reading a book.
Kipper came in and they sat on Biff's new carpet.
Kipper was learning to read and he wanted to
read to Biff.

Suddenly, the magic key began to glow.
Another adventure had begun. This time Biff and
Kipper were on a flying carpet.

"This is a new kind of adventure," said Biff.
"The carpet is coming with us."

The carpet went very fast.

"Oh help," said Kipper. "I hope we don't
fall off."

The carpet flew on and on. It flew over deserts
and mountains.

"I wonder where we're going!" said Biff.

At last, the carpet slowed down. Biff and
Kipper looked over the side. The carpet was
flying over a town.

"I've never seen a town like this one," said Biff.
"I wonder if we're going to land."

But the carpet didn't land. Instead it went
slower and slower. Then it stopped by a window
at the top of a tower.

"I wonder why we've stopped here," said Kipper.

Biff and Kipper looked through the window.
They saw a little boy. He was crying and he
looked very unhappy.

"He must be a prisoner," said Biff.

Biff and Kipper climbed into the little room.
When the boy saw them, he jumped up in
surprise.

"Why are you locked up in this tower?" asked
Biff. "What have you done?"

"I am the real king of this land," said the boy
sadly, "but my wicked uncle locked me in this
tower.

"When I was king everyone was happy.
I promised to rule the country wisely and well.
But my uncle was jealous. He wanted to be the
king, instead.

"One day my uncle and his soldiers attacked the palace. They captured me and put me in prison. My mother escaped. She ran away to the mountains and took her army with her.

"My uncle is a bad man. He is cruel and greedy. He makes the people pay him money even if they are poor. If they can't pay, he puts them in prison. Nobody is happy.

"Every day the people ask my mother and her army to attack the city. She will not give the order to attack because she is afraid my uncle will harm me. I am a hostage in this palace."

"Then we must set you free," said Biff. "The carpet will take us to your mother."
Biff and Kipper helped the boy to climb out of the window. Then they all sat on the carpet.

"How do we make it fly?" asked Kipper. "How will it know where to take us?"

"Make a wish," said Biff. "Then it'll go where we want it to."

They made a wish, and the carpet zoomed off.

The carpet sped towards the mountains. At
last it began to slow down.

"I hope it knows how to land," said Kipper.
"It looks a long way down."

The carpet landed safely. When the boy's
mother saw him, she couldn't believe her eyes.
She looked at the carpet and she looked at Biff
and Kipper.

"My son is safe," she said, "thank you."

The boy's mother called all her soldiers. She told them her son was free.

"Now he is safe, we can attack the city," she said. "My son will be king again."

"Hooray!" shouted the soldiers. They came
down from the mountains and marched to the city.
There was a big battle. Biff, Kipper and the boy
watched the battle from a safe place.

When the battle was over everyone was pleased that the boy was king again. But the boy was not pleased.

"Where is my uncle?" he asked. "He must be punished for what he did."

Biff and Kipper saw someone running away.
It was the wicked uncle.

"Oh no!" said Kipper, "he's getting away.
How can we stop him?"
Biff had the magic carpet with her.

"I wonder if...?" she thought.

Biff made a wish and the magic carpet flew
after the wicked uncle. The wicked uncle rode as
fast as he could but the carpet was faster.

"Stop him!" called Biff.

The carpet pulled the wicked uncle from his horse. It wrapped itself round him and then it rolled him back to the city.

"Help! Help!" called the wicked uncle. "Get this carpet off me!"

Biff and Kipper took the wicked uncle to the boy.

"Thank you," he said. "It's my uncle's turn to go to prison. Now I can be a good king and look after my people again."

The boy gave Biff and Kipper a present. It
was a beautiful toy camel.

"Thank you," they said.

Suddenly the magic key began to glow.

"It's time for us to go," said Biff, "but we'll
take our carpet if you don't mind."

The magic key took Biff and Kipper home.

"What an adventure!" said Kipper. "Do you think if I wish very hard, the carpet will take me to school each day?"

"You'll be lucky!" said Biff.